Space Mates

**Based on an original story by
Kate Jacoby**

Ginn is a registered trademark of Harcourt Education Ltd

Linacre House, Jordan Hill, Oxford, OX2 8DP
a division of Harcourt Education Ltd

www.myprimary.co.uk

Help and support, plus the widest range of education solutions

Space Mates © Kate Jacoby 2000

From the Spinouts project developed by Paul Collins and Meredith Costain.

This book is copyright and reproduction of the whole or part without the publisher's written permission is prohibited.

08 07 06 05 04
10 9 8 7 6 5 4 3 2 1

ISBN 0602 241138

Illustrated by Phil Garner and Shaun Tan
Cover illustration by Marc McBride
Designed by Carolyn Gibson
Repro by Digital Imaging, Glasgow
Printed and bound in Great Britain by Ashford Colour Press, Hants, UK

Kate Jacoby

Kate Jacoby has spent many years travelling the world. She lives in Melbourne, Australia, with her dog. Their house is surrounded by noisy birds.

About the story

"I grew up playing in the countryside behind my house with other kids from my street. I had the world's best hideout!"

Kate Jacoby

CHAPTER 1

The Not-So-Secret Hideout

Splat!

A big wet tanner nut came flying towards me. I was lucky this time – it hit the tree where I was hiding. I stayed behind the tree, out of the way.

My secret hideout was the best one for miles around. Well, it *was* a secret hideout – until yesterday. Someone went and told Vax all about it.

Vax was a bully. He and his gang had to have all the best things – so of course they wanted my hideout. And they would do anything to get it.

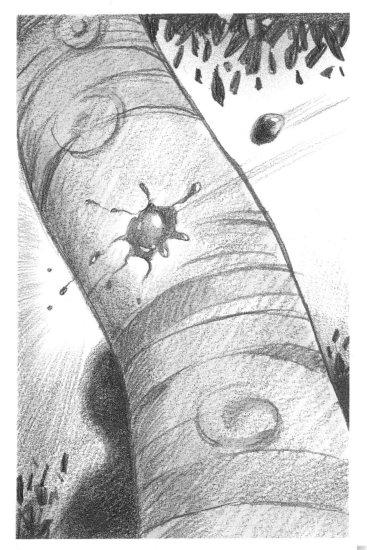

The rules said that a gang couldn't take over a hideout with someone still in it. So I wasn't going to leave. I didn't care if I missed dinner. My hideout was *mine*. I made it myself. I wasn't going to give it up for Vax and his gang of bullies. No way!

I looked up at my hideout, up in the top branches of the tree. Just then, I heard a spaceship roar across the sky. It was my dad coming in to land. I could tell it was him because his ship was the only one with blue stripes. I liked those stripes. When I saw them, I always knew it was Dad flying up there.

"Hey, Caca!" Vax yelled. "You know you've got to give up! Why don't you just give us your hideout?"

"I don't have to give up!" I shook my head crossly. "I know the rules better than you. If I stay here till dark, you can't take it."

"Well, maybe we'll just take it anyway!" Vax's friends laughed.

"You can't!" I said – but I knew they *could* take it, if they wanted to. What was I going to do?

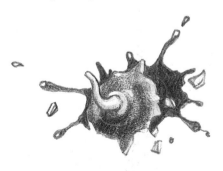

CHAPTER 2

Stinky Waka Berries

I heard Vax's gang laughing again, so
I peeped out. That was a big mistake!
At once, something hit me on the
side of the head. Something soft and
squashy. Stinky water went all over
me. Yuck! It was a waka berry.

"Stinky Caca! Stinky Caca!" Vax
shouted. His gang all started
laughing as if he had said something
really clever.

"Hey, Stinky!" yelled Vax's friend
Bo. "Do you think your dad will let
you sit in his ship smelling like that?"

"Stinky Caca doesn't even know about waka berries!" shouted Vax. "Don't they have waka berries where you come from?"

Every time Dad and I moved to a new place, kids like Vax tried to pick on me for being different. I wanted to yell back at him, but what was the point? Vax wasn't going to listen. He just wanted my hideout.

I looked up at my hideout. It was a long way up. I could almost see my store of waka berries. There was no way I could climb up to get them without getting hit.

"Hey, Stinky," said Vax again. "If you give me your hideout now, I'll let you go home in one piece. OK?"

"Go away!" I shouted. The waka berry smelt really bad now. I tried to work out what to do next. Then I noticed that Vax's gang had gone quiet. I peeped round the tree.

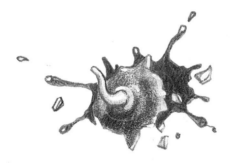

CHAPTER 3

The Alien Kid

A kid was standing there. At least,
I think it was a kid. It was an alien.
Of course, I had seen lots of aliens,
but never one like this.

The alien had brown stuff on top of its big head, and its eyes were way too close together. Its arms were long and dangly, and its feet were tiny. Its skin was very pale.

The alien was looking at me.

"Hey!" Vax shouted to the alien. "Get out of the way. Come over and join us, and you won't get hurt."

The alien kid switched on its translator machine. Then it turned to look at me.

"Do you want some help?" the kid asked. Its face looked so odd I almost laughed. But Dad had told me not to laugh at strange aliens.

The kid walked over and sat down next to me. Its legs were really

strange, but I tried not to stare.

"I had a hideout at home," said the kid. "My brother pulled it down."

"Oh," I said. "Hey – can you climb?"

"Sure," said the kid. "Why?"

"I'm slow at climbing. I've got waka berries up in the hideout, but if I go, I won't get to them in time."

The kid nodded. "It's not very far. I could climb up and throw berries down at them." In a flash, the alien grabbed a branch and started to climb. Soon it had reached the hideout and was out of sight.

CHAPTER 4

Alien Friends

Vax and his gang were standing right in front of me.

Splat! The first waka berry hit them.

"Ow!" Bo yelled as a berry hit him on the head. Vax tried to get out of the way, but he got hit too. Bo and Vax looked at each other, then ran off. The others ran after them, yelling.

That was the last I saw of them.

I waited for a bit, to make sure they were gone. Then I climbed slowly up to join my new friend. The alien kid was waiting for me, holding a waka berry.

"These are great for throwing!" said the kid.

"That's why we use them," I said. "Thanks for helping."

"Hey," said my friend. "Let's go and get some more berries in case Vax comes back."

"Good idea." I was going to like
this kid. "Have you been here long?"
I asked.

"We just got here yesterday," said
the kid. "My mother works at the
space port."

"My dad works there too – he flies a spaceship," I said. "So, what planet are you from?"

"Earth." I think the kid was smiling, but the smile looked different on an alien face.

"Really?" I'd never met someone from Earth before. "So are you a human?" I asked.

"That's right," said the Earth kid. "What about you?"

"My name is Calcania," I said. "I come from Rigel."

"I'm Lucy," said the Earth kid. "It's great to meet an alien who's so friendly!"

"What do you mean, an alien?" I said. "*You're* the alien."

"Maybe we both are," said Lucy. "I'm an alien to you, and you're an alien to me."

And we both smiled.